Let's Talk About TREES!

ROOPA PAI

Illustrated by Barkha Lohia

JUGGERNAUT BOOKS
C-I-128, First Floor, Sangam Vihar, Near Holi Chowk,
New Delhi 110080, India

First published by WWF-India 2023

This edition published by Shashthi Media and Juggernaut Books 2024

Copyright © WWF-India 2024

10 9 8 7 6 5 4 3 2 1

P-ISBN: 9789353452902
E-ISBN: 9789353452544

All rights reserved. No part of this publication may be reproduced, transmitted, or stored in a retrieval system in any form or by any means without the written permission of the publisher.

Disclaimer: The maps in the book are not to scale and do not depict the political boundaries accurately.

This book was created under the "Project Mission Million Trees" supported by Capgemini, to generate awareness among children about the ecological importance of planting native trees and improving green cover.

Printed at Replika Press Pvt Ltd
Written by Roopa Pai
Illustrated by Barkha Lohia
Art director and designer: Maithili Doshi

SubhAshita

छायां अन्यस्य कुर्वन्ति तिष्ठन्ति स्वयं आतपे ।
फलन्त्यपि परार्थाय वृक्षा: सत्पुरुषा इव ॥

chhAyAm anyasya kurvanti tishThanti svayam Atape |
phalAntyapi parArthAya vrukshAh satpurushA iva ||

They give shade while themselves standing in the heat of the sun—
And even bear fruit for others to enjoy—such noble beings are trees!

'Greening the earth is my sword to fight
for a better life—make it yours.'

—Saalumarada Thimmakka,
Indian environmentalist and Padma Shri awardee
famous for single-handedly planting and nurturing 387
banyan trees on a 4-km stretch of highway in Karnataka,
speaking to schoolchildren at the age of 107

Hello, hello, hello! Welcome to the amazing, extraordinary, mind-blowing TREEVERSE!

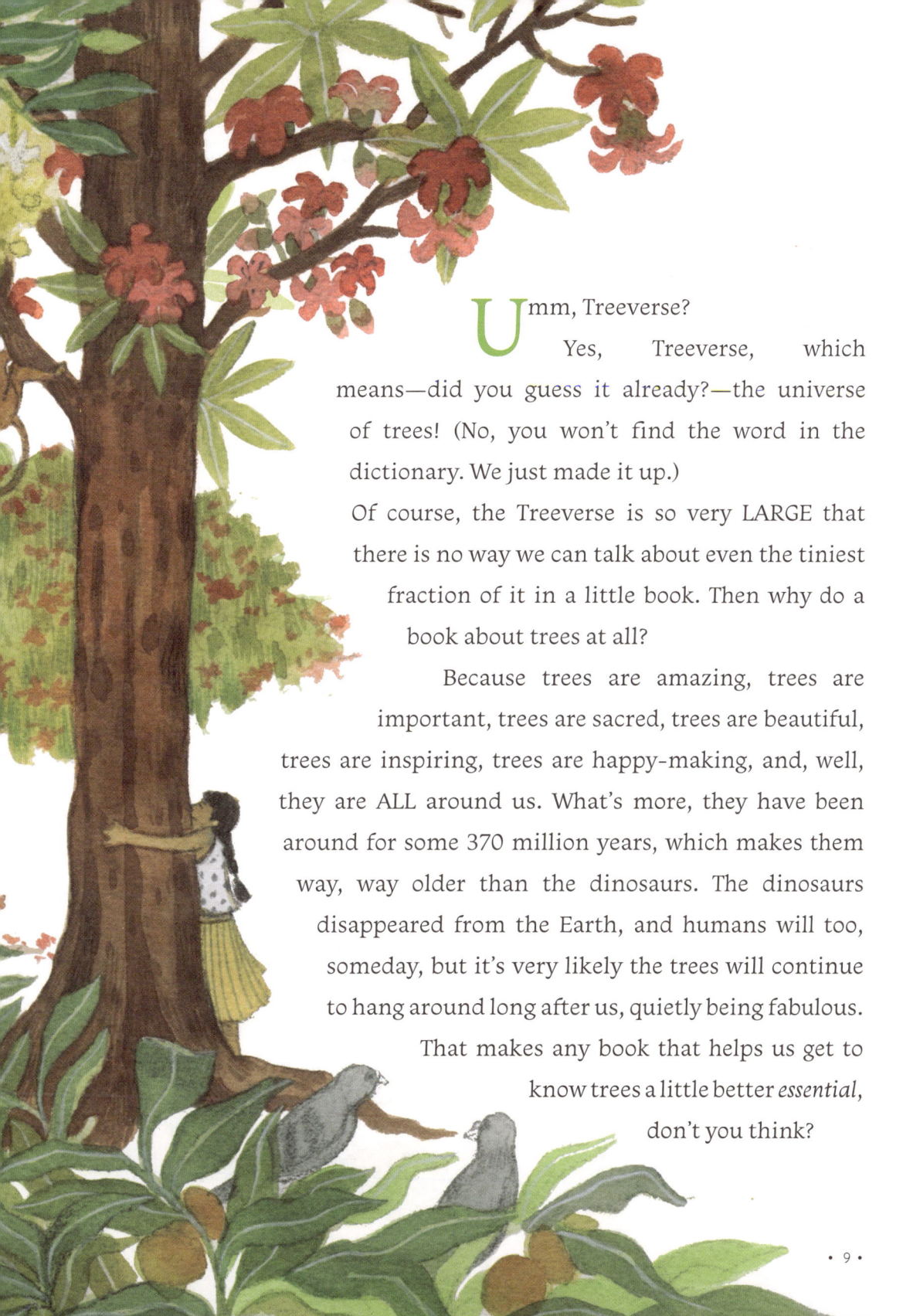

Umm, Treeverse?

Yes, Treeverse, which means—did you guess it already?—the universe of trees! (No, you won't find the word in the dictionary. We just made it up.)

Of course, the Treeverse is so very LARGE that there is no way we can talk about even the tiniest fraction of it in a little book. Then why do a book about trees at all?

Because trees are amazing, trees are important, trees are sacred, trees are beautiful, trees are inspiring, trees are happy-making, and, well, they are ALL around us. What's more, they have been around for some 370 million years, which makes them way, way older than the dinosaurs. The dinosaurs disappeared from the Earth, and humans will too, someday, but it's very likely the trees will continue to hang around long after us, quietly being fabulous. That makes any book that helps us get to know trees a little better *essential*, don't you think?

You see, it's only when you KNOW something that you can begin to LOVE it.

When you LOVE a tree, it will stop being something that simply exists and become something that LIVES, not only outside of you but inside you. Once you love one tree and make it your friend, you will begin to look at ALL trees differently, noticing quirky little details about each that you had never done before. You will feel deeply for every tree and want to celebrate each one's awesomeness. And that's a win, for you will never be lonely—or bored—as long as you have trees you love around you.

Look!
Listen!
LOVE!

Ready to plunge into the Treeverse now? Let's go! Before we begin, a quick question: **Have you looked at a tree recently?**

Don't make that 'Eh what? Are you sure you are quite all right?' face. It isn't *such* a weird question. The thing is, there is a great difference between looking at something and seeing something—when you 'look' at something, you observe it closely, noting the BIG and not-so-big and teeny-tiny details about it; when you 'see' something, you merely register its presence.

If you have really *looked* at a tree, any tree, you would have noticed many things about it. Things like its:

Trunk

The many-trunked crepe myrtle

🍃 Straight or twisty? Stout or slender? Single or multiple (yes, many trees do have multiple trunks!)?

The buttressed gulmohar

🍃 Large bottomed, because of the 'buttress' roots supporting the trunk (usually because the tree is not deeply rooted and will fall if not supported)? Or slim around the base (because the tree's roots go deep into the earth and can hold it strong and steady in a storm all by themselves?

Bark

🍃 Smooth or rough? Dark or light? Flaky and peeling, or even and unbroken? Sleek and glossy, or cracked and matt-finished?

The peeling bark of the guava

🍃 Shiny with sticky sap or dry and 'clean'? Prickly with thorns (ouch!) or velvety with moss? Creased and furrowed, or smooth and unwrinkled?

🍃 Red or brown or white or black?

The 'crocodile bark' of the matti

Branches

🍃 Does the trunk start branching close to the ground or wayyyyy higher up?

The low-branching mango

The 'let's-branch-sideways' baobab

🍃 Do the branches reach for the sky or grow out sideways?

How thick are the branches? How do the branches 'branch out' further?

Canopy (or the leafy 'crown' of the tree)

The floppy-crowned coconut

🍃 Highhhhhh up or low-ish? Vast and sprawling, or small and contained? Floppy like a coconut tree's or upstanding like a poplar's?

🍃 So dense that no sunlight reaches the ground under the tree and nothing can grow under it? Or light and airy, with spaces that sunlight can peek through, so that the tree casts a lovely dappled shade on the grass below?

And so on.

Plus, what are the leaves like—shape, colour, size? What colour are the fresh new leaves (they aren't always green, by the way) and what colour the old, dying ones?

Are there flowers? What kind? Do they smell nice?

Are there fruits or berries? Can you see seed pods? What do *they* smell like?

Can you spot birds' nests? Beehives? Upside-down bats?

So, once again: Have you LOOKED at a tree recently?

Yes? Then turn to page 21, fill in the blanks, and create a vivid word portrait of your tree, from memory.

No? Then go out into your garden, the street, the park, anywhere that you can find a tree, and LOOK at it. NOW. Don't forget to take this book with you (word portrait, remember?).

Go on then!

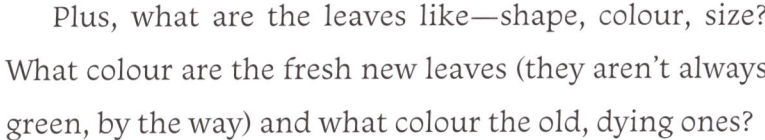

The shade of the sprawling Mysore fig plays peekaboo with the sun

I think I shall never see.
A poem lovely as a tree.*

Pick a tree, any tree, close to where you live. Sit down comfortably, at some distance from the tree, and observe it. (Turn the page to see what details you need to look for.) Spend at least 5 to 10 minutes simply sitting in silence and taking it in, from the very top to the very bottom. You may even want to walk around the tree, observing it from different angles.

The nicest part about observing trees, as compared to birds, animals, or insects, is that it's so easy to do! Trees do not fidget, scurry away, bite, or snarl at you. They stand around patiently and let you enjoy them to your heart's content—not just for an hour or two, but for years and years.

* These are the opening lines of what is probably the world's most famous poem in English about trees. It was written in 1913 by American poet Joyce Kilmer. Look for the rest of the poem on the Internet.

Right. Now, walk up to the tree and take a closer look. Use all your senses to know your tree—**see** it (the shape it makes, the form of its boughs), **observe** all the little organisms on it (ants, beetles, lichens, fungi), **feel** it (bark, leaf, flower, seed—they all have different textures), **smell** it (crush a freshly fallen leaf, sniff a flower—oh, but be careful if you have a pollen allergy!), **hear** it (leaves rustling, birds calling, wind whispering), **taste** it (uhhh, maybe skip this one). Don't forget to look below for fallen flowers and fruits and seeds and seed pods—trees are usually so tall that you can't really take a close look at these when they are still on the branches. Sketch or take pictures of fallen tree souvenirs for a scrapbook or display.

All done? Now begin to construct your word portrait!

Look at the form on the facing page. The first entry, 'Date and season', is really important. Trees look different in different seasons—they burst into flower in a certain month (if they are flowering trees), drop their leaves in a different month, and come into fruit in some other month. Observe your tree through the year (this is why it is important to pick a tree growing close by) and record the changes you see.* Taking a photograph (or making a drawing), every time you see a significant change, will help you do this better.

Oh, one last thing. Think of a name for your tree.

A name? But don't trees already have names—tamarind, neem, peepal? Sure, but you may not always know your tree's 'official' name. And guess what? It doesn't matter! Eventually, you can ask someone what it is called or look it up on the Internet. But until then, as long as you're getting to know your tree and making friends with it, you can give it ANY name that you think is appropriate, based on the look and feel of its trunk (crocodile skin tree, maybe?), the shape of its flowers (white trumpet tree, perhaps?), or its attitude (too-cool-for-school tree, why not?).

Don't stop at one tree. Do this look-observe-make-a-word-portrait exercise with two more trees, or five, until you have an entire cohort of tree-friends that are *yours*. If you like to sketch, make illustrations of your tree-friends to accompany their word portraits.

Off you go now, to make your first tree-friend!

---

* There's a way to do this officially! You get to not only track your tree's progress through the seasons but also share that information with other people, including serious scientists, who are also interested in trees. Just register yourself (and your tree) with Nature Conservation Foundation's (NCF) SeasonWatch and upload your findings there each week. This is an all-India program that tracks climate change by how and when different species of trees are flowering, fruiting, coming into leaf, and all the rest of it, so your inputs are very valuable.

My Tree Friend
A Word Portrait

- Date and season: _____

- My name(s) for my tree-friend: _____

- My tree-friend's official name: _____

Use three to five adjectives to describe each tree 'part' below.

- Trunk: _____

- Bark: _____

- Branching: _____

- Leaves: _____

- Flowers (if any): _____

- Fruits (if any): _____

- Seeds and seed pods (if any): _____

- Living things that my tree supports: _____

- What makes my tree special: _____

Make a Clay Leaf Bowl!

You need:

- A pack or two of air-drying clay (available in craft shops and online)
- Leaves of different shapes and sizes (don't pluck them, pick them off the ground)
- Rolling pin
- Bowl
- Small plate with a rim
- Gold paint and paintbrush

Make it!

- With the rolling pin, roll out your clay to a slab 1 cm thick.
- Press the upturned bowl on it to cut out a disc. Keep aside.
- Pour some gold paint into your rimmed plate.
- Pick a leaf from your collection and press it face down into the gold paint.
- Press the leaf, gold side down, into your clay disc.
- Press the disc, gold leaf side up, into the bottom of the bowl so that it gets a bowl shape.
- With the paintbrush, paint the rim of the clay bowl gold.
- Leave aside to dry for 24 hours before tipping the clay bowl out.

Ta-daa!

Now, What Exactly is a Tree?

Before you read on, spend a moment (or five) thinking about YOUR answer(s) to the question 'What exactly is a tree?'. Maybe you could scribble your thoughts down in your Tree Journal. Done? Super. You may now proceed to the official definitions. (For your Tree Journal, pick a notebook that has plain pages on one side and lined pages on the other. Use the plain side to sketch leaves, seed pods and so on, and the lined side to write down your observations. You can even use the plain side to make an occasional bark rubbing.)

We can all agree that a tree is essentially a plant. Like most plants, trees are rooted in the soil, from where they suck up water and minerals. Like most plants, they put out green leaves that have the ultimate superpower—turning the Sun's energy into food, for themselves and every other creature in the world! Plus, like plants, trees never stop growing through their entire lives—new leaves, new branches, buds, flowers, fruits...

But is the opposite true? Is a plant essentially a tree? Not quite! A tree, therefore, is a rather special kind of plant.

A tree is both:

- A **perennial plant** (i.e., a plant that lives for more than two years) that is at least 5 m tall when fully grown, and has an **elongated** stem (or trunk) that bears **branches** and **leaves.** (According to this definition, is a banana plant a tree?)

And...

- A **woody plant** that not only grows **taller** but also **thicker** throughout its life. (Do humans also experience both kinds of growths *throughout their lives*? Or neither?) According to this definition, a banana plant is NOT a tree because it does not have a woody stem. Can you think of any other plants that would not be considered trees even though they *look* like trees?

Let's Talk About Trees! • 25 •

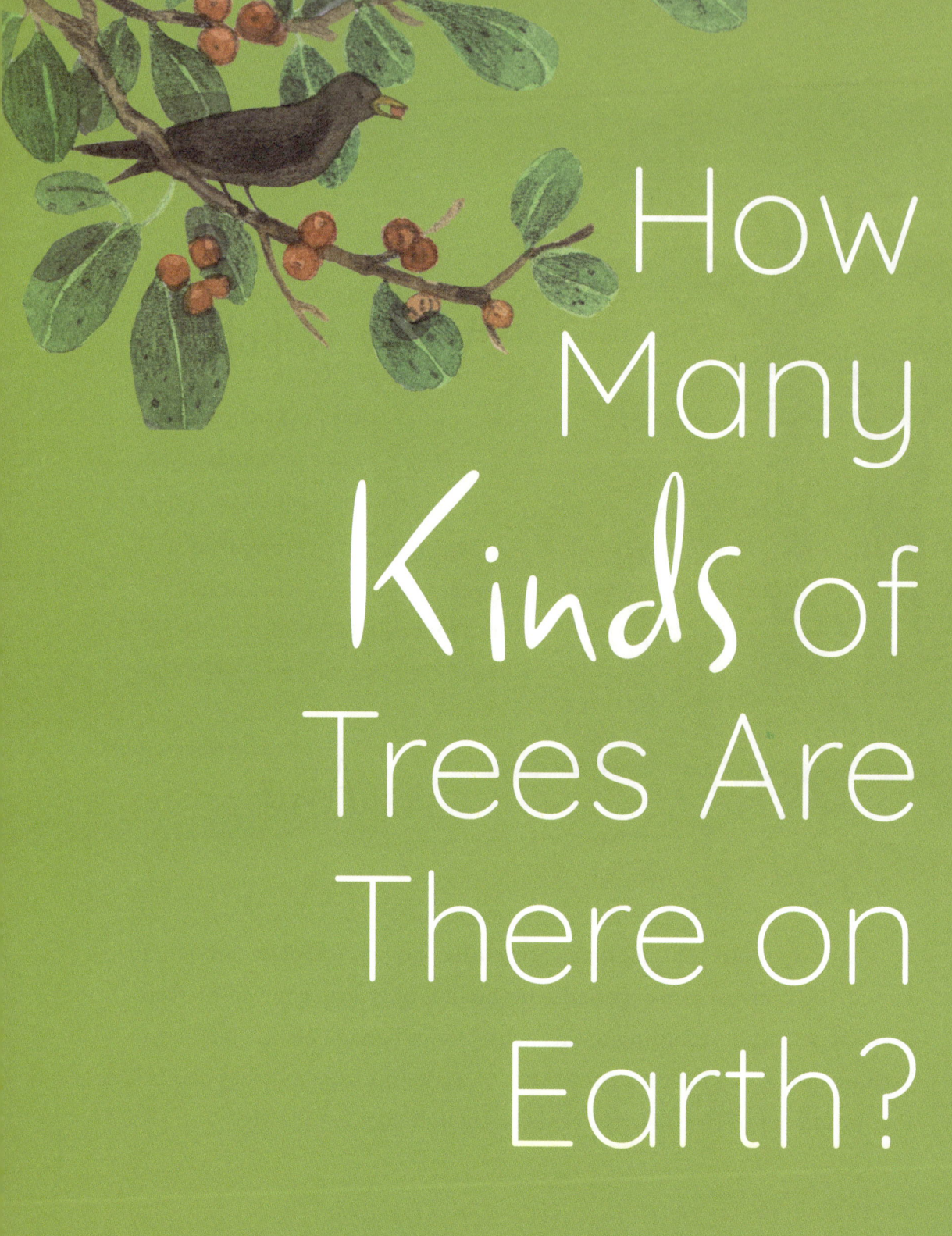

How Many Kinds of Trees Are There on Earth?

Whoa, tough question. There are thousands and thousands of kinds of trees—the latest estimate, which appeared in the January 2022 issue of PNAS (Proceedings of the National Academy of Sciences), a very respected American journal of original research, has the number at around 73,000 different species worldwide, of which a large number are still to be described! India alone has over 2,600 species.

Fortunately for all of us, scientists classify ALL trees into only TWO main types—evergreen and deciduous.

The difference between the two is very straightforward.

- **Evergreen** trees keep their leaves throughout the year.
- **Deciduous** trees drop their leaves every year, usually in a specific season. Some trees shed their leaves and stay bare through the winter months, and grow a fresh new crown in the spring, while some shed their leaves towards the end of winter, and burst into new green leaf a short two weeks later.

Image below: The number of tree species per continent in the database of the Global Forest Biodiversity Initiative (GFBI).

Adapted from:
Cazzolla Gatti R, Reich PB,
Gamarra JGP, et al.: The number of tree species on earth.
Proc Natl Acad Sci U S A. 2022; 119(6) e2115329119

In between these two, there are the **semi-evergreen** trees, which keep their leaves on when the winter is mild, but may drop them when the winter is harsh. Or they may drop their leaves only for a few weeks instead of many months. The same species of tree also may behave differently in different regions because of differences in soil, nutrition, and climate. Hmm, not so straightforward after all, eh?

After you have observed and recorded your tree-friends for a whole year, you will be able to tell which ones are evergreen, semi-evergreen, and deciduous.

Now imagine introducing your tree friend to your human friend: 'Hey Arnab, this is my friend HeartLeaf. She is a semi-evergreen. HeartLeaf, meet Arnab. A most interesting fact about HeartLeaf, Arnab, is that her fruits are hollow, and her flowers line the inside of the fruits! Most people call her, um, Peepal, haha...' (To find out more about the peepal, turn to page 60.)

What Do Trees Eat? And How?

They have no mouths, no stomachs, and no way to go from place to place looking for food. And yet, trees are some of the most ginormous living creatures on Earth. What exactly do they eat that makes them so big and strong?

A tree's staple diet—not even kidding—is sugar! But trees don't go around looking for sugar; they simply make their own. For their patented recipe, turn the page!

Ingredients

Water and carbon dioxide (CO_2)

along with

sunlight, and a pigment called chlorophyll, found in green leaves

Method

🍃 Expose your green leaves to sunlight, so that the chlorophyll can get to work, absorbing the Sun's energy.

🍃 Zap the water molecules in the leaves with that energy, so that the water splits into hydrogen and oxygen. [How does water get to the leaves? The tree's roots suck in water from the soil and send it upwards through the trunk and branches to every leaf, through special water-transporting cells that make up the xylem (say *zy-lem*)].

🍃 Combine the hydrogen with carbon dioxide and mix well. *Ta-daa!* Your sugar is ready! (Where did the carbon dioxide come from? From the air! The leaves breathed it in through tiny holes on their underside, called stomata.)

🍃 Clean up your leaf kitchen. Spit out the oxygen released from the water molecules back into the air through the stomata, and flush the extra water out as water vapour, so that fresh water can come in.

🍃 Send the warm, yummy sugar off to your branches, trunk, and roots via special sugar-transporting cells just inside the bark, called phloem (say *flow-em*).

🍃 Go back to the first step and repeat until the sun is gone. ('*Photo*' is the Latin word for light. To 'synthesize' means to make. That's why the fancy name for a tree's process of sugar-making is 'photosynthesis', or 'making in the presence of light'.)

When herbivorous or omnivorous animals and humans eat leaves and fruits, they bring the Sun's energy, which is vital for life, into their bodies. And carnivores? How do *they* imbibe solar energy? By eating the herbivores, of course! See how all of us need trees and plants to do what they do so that we can all be filled with life-giving energy?

Green leaves, as we just found out, are miniature power stations generating vital energy. Leaves can be tiny, h-u-g-e, long, narrow, broad, lobed (which means 'having two or more rounded or pointed parts that stick out from the main part'), glossy, furry, smooth-edged, jagged-edged, symmetrical, asymmetrical, multicoloured, and many other kinds of exciting shapes and types.

Botanists classify leaves into only two broad types, however—simple and compound. There are many technical differences between the two, and it is sometimes difficult to know if you are looking at a leaf or a leaflet. But here is a good way to start telling them apart:

🍃 A **simple leaf** has a single leaf blade attached to a twig or branch by a stalk. It is not divided into smaller leaflets (although it may have two or more lobes).

🍃 A **compound leaf** is a bunch of leaflets, each with its own stalk. Each leaflet is attached to a main stem, which in turn is attached to a twig or branch of the tree.

Confused? Just take a look at the illustrations and it will all become crystal clear!

Simple Leaves

But Seriously, Why Does Everyone Make Such a Tree-Mendous Deal about Trees?

But seriously, why don't you find out for yourself, by solving the puzzles below? Here goes.

1. Trees are humungous in every way! They are among the tallest and heaviest living creatures on Earth, live for hundreds of years, grow all over in the world in all kinds of environments, and there are SO MANY of them. The Earth has approximately 3,000,000,000,000, or THREE __ __ __ __ __ __ __ (what do you call a number with TWELVE zeros behind it? Clue: It has a close connection with TRees!) trees. In other words, they are **literally** a BIG deal!

2. The air we breathe is composed of a lot of _ _ _ _ _ _ (a gas that we need to stay alive) and very little _ _ _ _ _ _ / _ _ _ _ _ _ _ (a gas that our body produces as waste and speedily removes). While trees breathe, they do the opposite. They take in _ _ _ _ _ _ / _ _ _ _ _ _ , and give out _ _ _ _ _ _ . What a perfect relationship! How would we survive without trees?

3. Our cars run largely on petrol and diesel. A lot of our electricity is produced from coal. We cook our food on stoves powered by natural gas. Coal, petrol, and natural gas are fuels which release carbon dioxide (CO_2) when they are burnt. When there is too much carbon dioxide in the atmosphere, the atmosphere heats up in a phenomenon called _ _ _ _ _ _ _ (another word for international) _ _ _ _ _ _ _ (opposite of cooling). By absorbing carbon dioxide, trees prevent this from happening. How, um, **cool**!

4. There's more! Guess where the coal, petrol, and natural gas that we cannot do without come from? Also from trees—old, old ones! Those trees, which died millions of years ago, even before the dinosaurs arrived, were buried deeper and deeper in the earth as time rolled by, still holding the Sun's energy within them. The heat and pressure of all the layers of earth lying on top of them turned those old trees into—*ta-daa!*— the three fuels we talked about, which are together called

___ ___ ___ ___ ___ FUELS. Yes, the 21st century is largely powered by ancient trees. Goosebumps!

5. The roots of trees grow deep and wide into the earth, looking for water and ___ ___ ___ ___ ___ ___ ___ ___ (Clue: a collective name for substances like calcium, potassium, iron, phosphorus and sodium, which help plants—and humans!—grow) to nourish the tree with. This deep, wide root system holds the soil around the tree firm, and prevents the topsoil, the most nutritious layer of the soil, from being carried away by wind and water, in a process called SOIL ___R___S___ ___N (Clue: the four blanks are all vowels). Without topsoil, we could not grow our food crops. Thanks, trees!

6. Trees also provide us with a whole bunch of other useful and lifesaving products—___ ___ ___ ___ ___ ___ ___ ___ (what we take to make us better when we are ill), ___ ___ ___ ___ ___ ___ (wood that we use in building and furniture), ___ ___ ___ ___ ___ ___ ___ ___ (what many people use to cook food or heat water or warm themselves on a winter's night), ___ ___ ___ ___ ___ (what this book is printed on), cool shade on a searing summer afternoon, a vast variety of fruit, flowers, spices, and oils, roof thatching for huts, heart-lifting sights, and so much more. Go hug a tree—now!

ANSWERS: 1. Trillion; 2. Oxygen, carbon dioxide, carbon dioxide, oxygen; 3. Global warming; 4. Fossil; 5. Minerals, Erosion; 6. Medicine, lumber (or timber), firewood, paper.

How Do Trees Stand So Straight and Tall When They Don't Even Have Backbones?

Good question! About 500 million years ago, plants, which had until then grown only in water, evolved to live on land. But it took them 130 million more years to figure out the engineering required to create a trunk that was strong enough to support the weight of an entire tree while 'standing up'.

Here are some cool innovations that trees came up with to make this possible.

🍃 They built their own 'backbones'

Trees grow in two ways. They grow **longer** at the tips of their roots (searching for water) and at the tips of their branches (searching for the sun). They also grow **thicker** around their trunks. Each year, when the weather is favourable, the trunk grows a new ring of cells and gets fatter. This new ring consists of xylem cells, which take over the job of moving the water and minerals from the roots to the leaves. The older ring of xylem dies, and joins the even older rings inside the trunk to become what is called the heartwood, the strong, solid centre of the tree.

(PS: It isn't quite accurate to call the heartwood of a tree its backbone, but it certainly does for the tree what our backbones do for us—keeps it upright.)

🍃 They figured out an anti-gravity transport system

To move water and minerals from their roots to their highest leaves, trees have to work very hard against gravity. We have a heart that works as a pump to move our blood from our feet to our chests and even higher, but trees don't. How do they do it, then? They use something called capillary action, a process in which liquids rise by themselves in very narrow tubes. It is capillary action that allows a paper towel or a sponge to suck up a spill, and capillary action that trees use to 'lift' water and minerals through xylem to the height of their highest leaves.

Now, we know that when a sponge is full of liquid, it will not absorb any more until you have squeezed it dry. What do trees do to 'squeeze themselves dry' so that new water and nutrients can come in? They 'transpire', or throw out extra water from their leaves continuously, in the form of vapour. Simple!

🍃 They grew bark

The hard, protective outer covering of a tree, bark is made up of layers and layers of dead cells that keep insects out, resist fire damage, and make sure the tree loses as little water as possible. Just inside the outer bark is the inner bark, made up of phloem, which transports

Archaeopteryx (Greek for 'old wing'), a bird-like dinosaur believed to be the ancestor of modern birds

Archaeopteris (Greek for 'old fern'), believed to be the first 'true' tree

sugar from the leaves to all parts of the tree (see why you need to be very careful not to cut into the bark of a tree?). Phloem only lives for about a year, after which the tree grows a new ring of phloem. The old, dead phloem gets pushed outwards, making the bark thicker and harder. This thick, hard bark also adds to the strength of the trunk. Double whammy!

Can You Really Tell the Age of a Tree by Counting its Rings?

Sometimes. But not always. Here's why.

When does a tree grow a ring of new cells inside its trunk? When the weather is favourable. In the world's temperate regions, where winters are harsh, trees grow in spring and summer. In their trunks, those seasonal growth spurts show up as a light-coloured ring of 'earlywood' when the trunk is fattening rapidly, and a dense, narrow, darker-coloured ring of 'latewood' when the weather starts getting cold and the trunk is fattening more slowly. (It's this darker border that makes growth rings so easy to see and count.) Then the tree stops growing thicker until the weather is favourable again.

What happens to trees that grow in the world's tropical regions, including much of India? They grow through the year, slowly and steadily, because the weather is *always* favourable. And that means... that's right, no dark latewood, and therefore, no clear rings! It's almost impossible to tell the age of trees like these, by looking at a cross-section of their trunks.

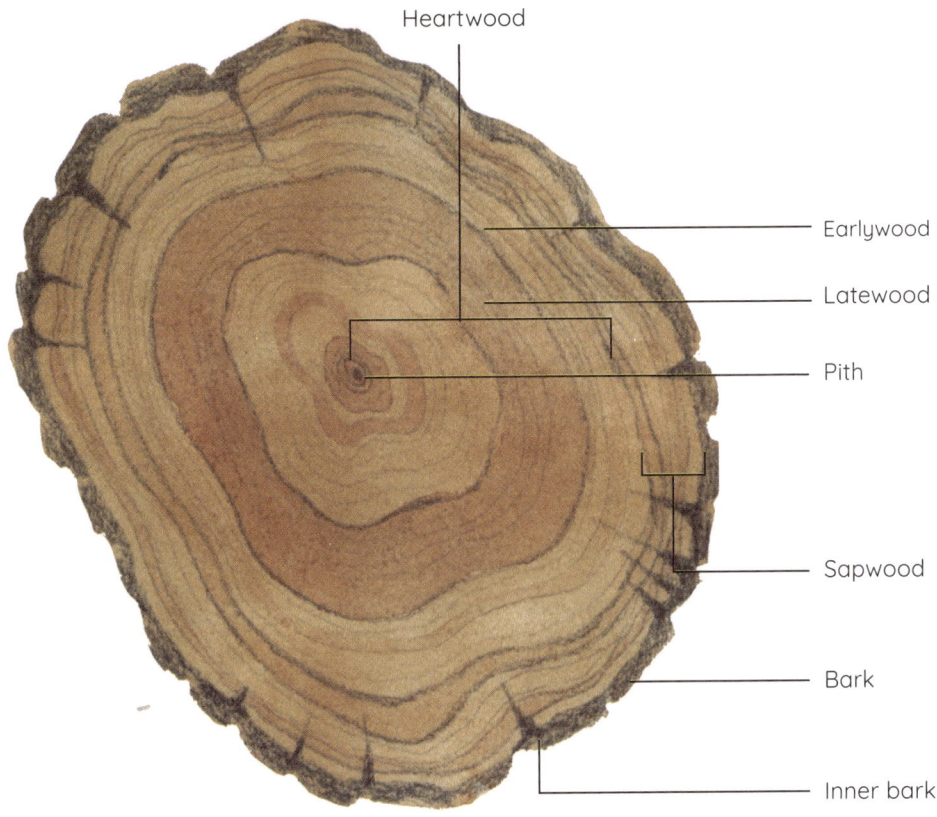

Even when a tree has rings, the number of rings may not be the most accurate way of telling its age. How come? Often, many annual rings are fused together, which makes it difficult to tell how many years they represent. There's another problem as well. In particularly dry years, when there isn't enough rainfall, or in years when the weather conditions are extreme—too hot or too cold— the tree may not grow thicker at all. Which means... yes, missing growth rings!

Estimate the Height of a Tree — by its Shadow, and Yours!

WHAT YOU NEED:

- A tree standing on a large expanse of level ground
- A sunny day
- A friend
- A tape measure
- A paper and pen (for calculations)

Let's estimate!

- Use the tape measure to measure your height in centimetres (cm). Write the number down on your paper, labelling it 'My height'.

- Stand at a spot where your shadow is clearly visible. Ask your friend to measure your shadow with the tape measure, from your heels (not toes!) to the tip (the topmost part of the shadow's head), also in cm. Write the number down against the title 'Length of my shadow'.

• Now measure the length of the shadow of the tree you have picked. (For a more accurate calculation, it is important to do this soon after you've measured your own shadow, because shadows change in length through the day.) Start from the base of the tree and go all the way to the top of its shadow. Record the height of the shadow in cm, against 'Length of tree's shadow'.

• Technically, this number is not quite accurate, because we should measure the tree's shadow from the **middle** of the tree's trunk, not from the edge. How can we do this? Draw a square or rectangle around the base of the tree, in which two sides are parallel to the tree's shadow. Measure one of the parallel sides, in cm, to give you an approximate diameter of the trunk. Halve this number to get the distance from the base of the tree to its centre.

- Add this number to the length of the tree's shadow and record the sum under 'TRUE length of tree's shadow'.

- Now for some more mathematics (use an adult's help to work this out if you can't do it yourself)! We have three numbers: your height, the length of your shadow, and the true length of the tree's shadow. There is only one unknown quantity—the tree's height. All you need to do now is use this formula to calculate it!

- Tree's height = My height (say, 140 cm) x Tree's shadow's TRUE length (say, 600 cm)/My shadow's length (say, 175 cm)

- We could then calculate the tree's height to be: 140 x 600 / 175 cm = 480 cm, or almost 16 feet (ft)*. Easy-peasy!

*16 ft is not very tall for a tree, but you get the idea.

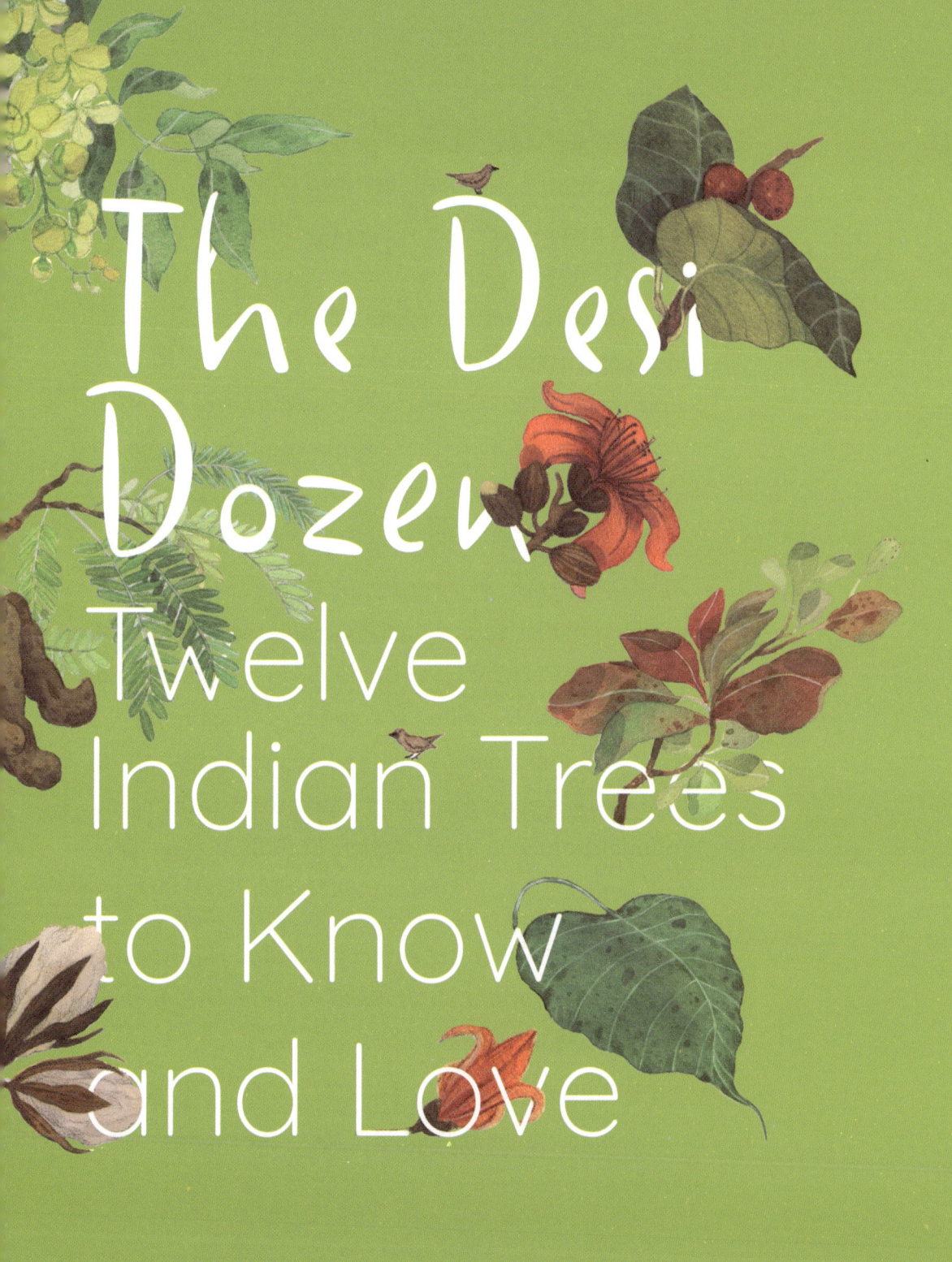

The Desi Dozen
Twelve Indian Trees to Know and Love

Before we dive in, a little detour to answer an important question: If different people have different names in different languages for the same tree, doesn't it all get a bit confusing? You bet it does—the Indian Constitution itself lists 22 languages as 'official languages', never mind the rest of the world! How do people—especially scientists—know which tree the other is talking about unless there is one standard name for it that everyone recognizes? It was a question that had troubled clever people through the ages.

Until, in the 18th century, 1753 CE to be precise, Swedish botanist and zoologist Carl Linnaeus put us all out of our misery by inventing a clean, elegant way of naming plants. He called his system of taxonomy (in Greek, taxonomy means 'method of arrangement'), in which every species was given a two-word Latin name, 'binomial nomenclature', (which literally means 'two-word name').

Here are a few 'Linnaean' names for Indian plants, along with a basic translation of their meanings. Roll them around your tongue and see how they feel!

What is the scientific name of:
- The mango tree? *Mangifera indica*—the mango of India.

- The banyan? *Ficus benghalensis*—the fig of Bengal.
- The mast tree (which we usually wrongly refer to as the Ashoka tree)? *Polyalthia longifolia*—the long-leaved tree that has many curative properties.
- The fragrant champaca? *Magnolia champaca*—the magnolia which is known as champaca. (Champaka is the name for this particular tree/flower in Telugu. Maybe the botanist who named it first noticed it in Andhra Pradesh?).
- The peepal? *Ficus religiosa*—the sacred fig (find out why on page 60).

See how much you can learn about a tree just by knowing its scientific name?

Oh, and what is our scientific name, as humans, according to binomial nomenclature? *Homo sapiens*—the wise man! Hmmm. Do you think, given the things we do and the way we behave, that that name is appropriate for our species?

PS: How about giving your own favourite tree or least-favourite fruit your own double-barrelled name, in whatever real or made-up language you choose? Here's an example. *Ugh, I hate the smell of jackfruit, so I have decided to christen it... umm... I know! Giganticus malodorous!*

BANYAN
The Tree That Walks

The splendid, sprawling banyan, or the Bengal fig, is a symbol of India itself, which is why we made it our national tree. It grows widely and luxuriantly across the country, taking root wherever birds drop its seeds after eating its fruit. In villages across India, for centuries, traders and moneylenders have conducted their business in its welcoming shade.

Cool facts

As the banyan's branches grow outwards from its trunk, they send roots towards the earth. Once these roots take root, they become as thick as trunks themselves, propping up the branch they came from. The supported branch can now grow even further out. This process keeps repeating until, years later, what started as ONE tree with ONE trunk grows into what looks like an entire forest of trees, covering a whole lot of ground. The original tree has 'walked' in every direction!

How to recognize a banyan
By its prop roots—you can't miss them!

Where you can spot them
Because of their vast, shady canopies, banyans have been planted along highways for hundreds of years. Look out for them on road trips!

India's Great Banyans

🌿 Thimmamma Marrimanu in Anantpur, Andhra Pradesh, is over 550 years old. Its canopy covers—hold your breath—4.7 acres!

🌿 The Great Banyan of Kolkata, with a perimeter of half a kilometre, is almost as big. Its canopy already covers 4.67 acres, and it is only 250 years old.

🌿 The Dodda Aalada Mara in Ramohalli outside Bangalore, with its spread of 2.5 acres, is a true-blue star. It was between its root-trunks that the iconic song *Yeh Dosti*, from the 1975 Bollywood classic film *Sholay*, was shot.

PEEPAL
The Tree of Wisdom

Like the banyan, the peepal is also a large fig species. It is often called the sacred fig*, because it is worshipped by Hindus and Buddhists. It is also called the Bodhi tree (or the tree of wisdom), because it is believed that Prince Siddhartha Gautama was meditating under one of these trees some 2,500 years ago when the solutions to the sorrows of the world were revealed to him, turning him into the Buddha (the Wise One).

Cool facts

Peepals live very, very long—their average lifespan is, reportedly, between 900 and 1,500 years! They can grow anywhere, and they are strong and hardy. If a peepal seed lodges itself into a small gap in a building wall, you can be sure that there will be a healthy plant growing out of it in a few days. As it wedges itself deeper into the wall, it may even end up cracking the wall. That's why the tree of wisdom is considered to have a high IQ—not 'intelligence quotient' but, 'invasiveness quotient'!

* Remember its botanical name from page 55?

But Seriously, Why Does Everyone Make Such a Tree-Mendous Deal about Trees?

But seriously, why don't you find out for yourself, by solving the puzzles below? Here goes.

1. Trees are humungous in every way! They are among the tallest and heaviest living creatures on Earth, live for hundreds of years, grow all over in the world in all kinds of environments, and there are SO MANY of them. The Earth has approximately 3,000,000,000,000, or THREE ___ ___ ___ ___ ___ ___ ___ (what do you call a number with TWELVE zeros behind it? Clue: It has a close connection with TRees!) trees. In other words, they are literally a BIG deal!

How to recognize a peepal

By its leaves, which have a very unique heart shape (remember 'Heartleaf' from page 29?) and a 'drip tip' for rain to slide off. Also, by its bark, which is brownish grey and flaky and peeling in patches. Peepal trees almost always have fluted, curving-in-and-out trunks (see illustration), which is another good way to identify them.

Where you can spot them

Everywhere! They are particularly common in the plains of India, but you can find them around Hindu temples and Buddhist shrines, and growing out of cracks in walls from seeds that birds have dropped there, anywhere in the country. In Karnataka, the *ashwattha katte*, or 'platform around the peepal tree', is part of village culture—it is where men and women meet to discuss politics, do business or simply have a chat.

India's most famous peepal

The Mahabodhi tree in Bodh Gaya, Bihar, is believed to be a descendant of the actual Bodhi tree under which the Buddha meditated 2,500 years ago! The tree is within the premises of the ancient Mahabodhi Temple originally built by Emperor Ashoka.

TAMARIND
The Ghost Host

Even though it came originally from Africa, the world has always associated the large tamarind tree, best known for its yummy, tangy, pucker-your-face fruit that all Indians love, with India. Its name comes from the Arabic *tamar-i-hind*, or *tamar indi*, which literally translates to 'Indian date'. Plus, India is the largest producer of tamarind in the world, most of which she consumes herself, in chutneys, sambar, *imli* candy and more.

Cool facts

The tamarind is a tall tree with a short, almost black, trunk. Its dense, heavy canopy, packed with tiny leaves, casts a dark, cool shade. This makes the ground underneath it cooler than the surroundings. Very little grows under the tamarind tree—not only because sunlight has a hard time getting through the canopy, but also because the soil is often acidic. Now imagine walking along a cemetery wall after dark, and shivering suddenly as you pass into the chill under a tamarind tree. This is probably why some people believe that ghosts live on tamarind trees!

How to recognize a tamarind

By its fruit, hanging down in bunches, encased in green-brown velvety pods. When it isn't fruiting season, look for other indicators, like the dark bark or the dense shade or the short trunk.

Where you can spot them

In and around cemeteries, haha. Also in parks, along avenues, and anywhere that people live, because the tamarind is more a planted tree than a wild one. You can spot the tamarind fruit in most Indian kitchens, and most certainly in the marketplaces of Chintamani, a town in Andhra Pradesh that is the largest trading centre for tamarind in the world!

Famous tamarinds

The tomb of Emperor Akbar's court musician, the great Mia Tansen, in Gwalior, is shaded by a large tamarind tree.

KHEJDI
The Wonder Tree of the Desert

What makes the khejdi (sometimes spelt as 'khejri') such a wonder? It can survive in hot, dry places where there is hardly any rain through the year. It thrives in temperatures as high as 50 °C and as low as 10 °C. It can take on the hottest winds without its leaves crisping up and crumbling into dust. Nourished by roots that sneak deep into the earth to look for water, it provides a large canopy of juicy, nutritious green leaves for camels, cattle, sheep, hares, blackbuck, and deer to chomp on. And this, in places where hardly any other trees grow!

In Rajasthan, the khejdi is a precious resource for humans as well. Its bark, which has many uses in medicine, including soothing scorpion bites, is also ground up into flour. The seed pods, called *sangri*, are cooked with *ker*, a dried berry, to make a delicious sweet-sour dish called *ker sangri*. Its timber is used to make camel carts and furniture. No wonder the khejdi is the state tree of Rajasthan, and a sacred tree to the Bishnoi people (read more about them on page 118).

Cool facts

Because the khejdi is constantly under attack by 'browsers' like cows and camels, it does a rather clever thing to protect itself—it builds its own 'fence'. While still a baby tree, it puts out horizontal branches in all directions, so that it is more a large, round bush than a tree. As the browsers help themselves to the leaves on the outside, the central stem thickens and grows tall and strong, eventually taking the leaves out of harm's reach.

How to recognize a khejdi

By its feathery leaves, with the tiny leaflets arranged in pairs on either side of a central stalk. Also look for the thorns on its branches—they form another level of protection from the browsers.

Where you can spot them

In dry, arid regions, and everywhere in the desert. The khejdi is also the national tree of the desert kingdom of the UAE, where it is called a ghaf.

Famous khejdis

The Tree of Life in the kingdom of Bahrain is a 400-year-old ghaf. It stands in the Arabian Desert, some 40 kms from Bahrain's capital, Manama, with its crown of fresh green leaves, never mind that there is no water for miles around it!

NEEM
Nature's Medicine Cabinet

Forgot to pack a toothbrush? Just grab a young neem twig and brush your teeth with it for a germ-free mouth! Feel regular soaps are loaded with harmful perfume and chemicals? Use one infused with natural neem (or margosa) oil, which is really good for your skin. Hate the thought of using chemical pesticides in your garden? Use neem oil and neem leaf extract as pesticide, and keep your plants—and pets—safe! Want to control diabetes? Chew on some bitter neem leaves each morning. Yes, the neem tree is an entire apothecary* unto itself!

Cool facts

In the states of Karnataka, Andhra Pradesh, and Telangana, the new year is celebrated in springtime, just when the neem is coming into flower. The joyous festival is called Ugadi. As part of the celebrations, people eat a mixture of bitter neem flowers, sour raw mango, and sweet jaggery, and tell themselves, 'Whatever the new year brings, bitter or sour or sweet, I will take them all in the same spirit.'

* person who made and sold medicines in earlier times

How to recognize a neem

By the serrated edges on its slender, light green leaves, which stand out against a dark bark marked by vertical furrows. In springtime, by its pretty sprays of small, fragrant white flowers, and in summer, by its small (about 2 cm long) bright yellow fruit.

Where you can spot them

In warm, dry places; neem can bear neither the cold nor waterlogging. Uttar Pradesh has the most neem trees, followed by Karnataka and Tamil Nadu. Neem is also the state tree of Andhra Pradesh.

A quick recipe for Baevu-Bella
(in Kannada, baevu is neem and bella is jaggery).

It's yummy, and you can make the mixture in neem flower season whether you celebrate Ugadi or not.

Mix together:
- ½ cup roasted gram (chutney dal), powdered
- ¼ cup neem flowers
- ¼ cup grated jaggery
- A fistful of chopped raw mango

Pop a tablespoon of the mixture into your mouth, and enjoy the burst of flavours. (The mix will keep for a week or more if you store it in the fridge.)

PALASH
The Flame of the Forest

People often mistakenly refer to the gulmohar as the 'flame of the forest'. But the gulmohar is a foreign tree from Madagascar, and it is more often found on Indian city streets than in the Indian forest. The palash, on the other hand, is usually found in deciduous forests. When it bursts into crimson bloom and drops all its leaves, the tree truly looks like it is on fire. This is a great time to observe the birds that come to sip the nectar in the flowers—because there are no leaves, you can see the birds clearly.

The palash flower has five petals, one of which is larger than the other four and curves upward, looking very much like a parakeet's red beak. That's why the palash is also called the parrot tree.

Cool facts

When palash flowers are soaked in water, the water turns a beautiful yellow. You can use this water to dye your clothes a wide range of colours from yellow to crimson, just like Buddhist monks have done for millennia! In fact, dried and powdered palash flowers were the original *'gulal'* that people used to play Holi.

🍃 What connects *puchka* (*pani puri/gol gappa*) with the palash? The leaf bowls in which streetside vendors serve them are stitched from palash leaves!

🍃 A very important battle in Indian history, which turned the British from traders to colonizers, was fought in 1757 in the town of Palashi, famous for its palash trees, in what was then Bengal. The name of the battle is very similar to the tree's. Can you guess which battle we are talking about? The Battle of Plassey, of course!

How to recognize a palash

In February and March, it is unmissable, with its canopy of flaming red flowers. In other seasons, look for the large, trifoliate (three leaves on one stalk), leathery leaves. (Palash leaves look a lot like teak leaves, but teak leaves are bigger and rougher. See page 88-89 to know how to tell with certainty if a leaf is a teak leaf).

Where you can spot them

All over the country, but particularly in the dry, deciduous forests of central and western India, particularly Jharkhand. No wonder the palash flower is the state flower of Jharkhand!

DEODAR

'Wood of the Gods'

Not even kidding—in Sanskrit, 'deodar' (which is how British botanists mapping India spelt it), or *'devadaar'* (which is how we refer to it in Hindi), literally means 'wood of the gods' (*deva*=god, *daru*=wood or tree). The deodar is a conifer, a class of evergreen trees that carry their seeds not in fruits but in cones. Part of the pine family, it is also called the Himalayan cedar, and is probably the longest-lived and tallest tree in India.

The deodar is super-popular with builders and carpenters. How come? Its wood is strong, and more importantly, termite-resistant. That's probably why it was called the wood of the gods in the first place!

Cool facts

- The deodar is the state tree of Himachal Pradesh, and the national tree of... Pakistan! (Yes, the western Himalayas, where the tree grows, sprawl over parts of Afghanistan, Nepal, Tibet, and Pakistan.)
- The famous, beautifully carved wooden houseboats that float along the edges of the Dal Lake in Kashmir are usually built of deodar wood.

🍃 A most useful insect-repelling, fungus-resisting oil is extracted from the deodar's inner wood.*

How to recognize a deodar

When it is young (deodars live for hundreds of years, so they are still young at 50), the deodar looks very much like a Christmas tree, with a conical top and drooping ends to its branches. As it grows older, and taller (it can grow as high as 50 metres (m), or the height of a 15-story building!), the top flattens out and the branches straighten up. The trunk of this magnificent tree can have a girth (or circumference) of up to three metres!

Where you can spot them

At altitudes of 1500 m to 3000 m, all over Jammu & Kashmir, Himachal Pradesh and Uttarakhand. If you are a Ruskin Bond fan, you've probably encountered this tree in his books—the slopes of his hometown of Mussoorie are full of them!

---

* Hmmm, where would YOU use such an oil? Write your ideas down before you check whether it is already being used in those ways. If not, you may have a winner on your hands!

KAPOK
The Silk Cotton Bearer

Ka-POK! Ka-POK! Is that a cute sound or what? You probably would not guess that it was the informal name of a giant tree (the formal, scientific name is *Bombax ceiba*, just FYI), but it is. The Indian kapok, also known as semal, grows in dry deciduous forests, which stretch from Khathiar-Gir (a region that covers parts of Gujarat, Rajasthan, and Madhya Pradesh) in the west to the Chhota Nagpur Plateau (which extends across Jharkhand, Chattisgarh, West Bengal, Bihar, and Odisha) in the east. In fact, Simlipal in Odisha is named after *simli*, the Odiya name for the semal!

Cool facts

- Kapok is actually the Malay word for the soft, silky fibre found inside the seed pod capsules of the silk-cotton tree. That natural fibre is used to stuff pillows and duvets, and lifejackets as well.
- The word *Bombax* in kapok's botanical name comes from the Latin *bombyx*, which means silkworm. Makes sense, given the silky floss the tree produces!
- Dried kapok flower buds are used as a special, little known spice called

marathi moggu in South Indian cooking. This spice is an essential ingredient in bisi bele bath, the favourite dish of Karnataka.

🍃 The oil pressed out from kapok seeds is very much like cottonseed oil. It is great for the skin, can be used for cooking, and helps relieve congestion when rubbed on the chest.

How to recognize a semal/kapok

Look for a b-r-o-a-d trunk, rough with cracks, and usually studded with hard prickles to keep monkeys from climbing it. Look for tall, thin, spreading buttresses (roots that prop up the tree from the ground). Look for palmate leaves, which usually have five leaflets each, like the five fingers of a human hand (see why this leaf shape is called palmate?). In March and April, look for red cup-shaped flowers with five petals, and a canopy full of birds that love the nectar in those flowers. In May and June look for the burst-open seed pods and the scattered silk-cotton floss at the bottom of the tree.

Where you can spot them

All over India, planted along city avenues and in parks, growing wild in forests and along the coast. Northeast India and West Bengal are full of kapok trees!

TEAK
The Grande Dame of the Indian Jungle

Did you know that 'teak' comes from the Malayalam name for the tree, tekka, which the Portuguese, when they arrived, turned into teca, which the British, who came later, turned into teak? Now you do! With its giant leaves and its cloud-cotton sprays of tiny, fragrant white flowers, the teak makes a pretty sight in the springtime. Its botanical name is more straightforward: *Tectona grandis*, the large tree that is the joy of carpenters (*tekton* is Greek for carpenter).

Why carpenters? Because teak wood is a favourite (and expensive!) material for making furniture, doors, window frames, and so much else. It has also been used for boat-building for centuries—in 1989, archaeologists discovered a 2000-year-old teak boat in the Sudan.

Cool facts

🌿 The two biggest living teak trees in the world, Homemalynn 1 & 2, were discovered only in 2017, in the Homalin township (see where the tree names come from?) of Myanmar. Homemalynn 1 is 34 m tall (about the height of a ten-storey building), and its trunk has a girth (or circumference) of—hold your breath—8.4 m!

🍃 Before the Homemalynns were discovered, Kerala held the record for the largest (read: thickest) living teak tree. In Palakkad's Parambikulam Tiger Reserve stands the over-450-year-old old matriarch, Kannimara/Connemara, much taller than Homemalynn 1 at 47.5 m, but just a little thinner in the trunk (7.15 m girth).

🍃 The oldest existing British warship is the HMS Trincomalee, now part of the Royal Navy Museum in Hartlepool, UK. She was built from teak, in 1812, in Mumbai, by the famous shipbuilding family from Surat, the Wadias.

How to recognise a teak

By its large, egg-shaped leaves, for one. But how can you be absolutely sure? Pick up a fallen leaf from the ground (or ask permission to pick one tender leaf from the tree), and crush and rub it between your palms. If your palms turn red from the leaf, it's a teak!

Where you can spot them

In forests all over the country! These days, you don't have to travel to a forest to spot them, however—they grow abundantly in teak plantations, where they are specially cultivated for their timber. (PS: The oldest 'planted teak' on Earth is Tree No. 23, which has stood in the world's first teak plantation, Conolly's Plot, in Nilambur, Kerala, since 1846.)

JACK
The World's Largest Fruit

The jackfruit is as Indian a tree as it gets—archaeologists have found evidence of jackfruit cultivation in India from 6,000 years ago! To this day, it remains a favourite in all its forms—in its unripe form, cooked into a curry; in its sweet, ripe form, eaten as a fruit; sliced and fried up into chips; or turned into a *payasam* with coconut milk. In 2021, India produced 1.8 million tonnes of jackfruit—way more than any other country in the world.

Cool facts

- Why is the jackfruit called a jackfruit? When the Portuguese explorer Vasco da Gama dropped anchor in Kozhikode in Kerala in 1497, he and his men were fascinated by this weird, large, smelly fruit covered all over in prickles. The locals called it *chakka*, which the Portuguese interpreted as jaca. At some point, it became jack. Simple!
- The jackfruit is the world's largest fruit, and each tree produces between 150 and 500 fruits a year! The branches would never be able to bear the weight of the fruits, so the tree bears them on its trunk.
- With veganism (a diet without meat or dairy products) becoming popular

with people across the world, the jackfruit is in high demand. How come? When cooked, jackfruit tastes very much like pork. People who want to be vegan but miss the taste of meat can now simply enjoy a 'pulled pork' jackfruit burger instead!

🍃 The jackfruit is the state fruit of TWO Indian states—Kerala and Tamil Nadu. It is also the national fruit of Bangladesh.

How to recognize a jackfruit

By the ginormous fruits hanging off its trunk, silly! But when it isn't fruiting season, look for a tree with a short trunk, a heavy canopy, a smooth reddish-brown bark, and thick, leathery, dark green leaves.

Where you can spot them

Growing wild all over the Western Ghats, but also in parks, home gardens, in farms along with other crops, and in plantations all over India.

BADAM
The Not-Quite-Almond

Its fruit—or more correctly, its seed—looks and tastes a lot like an almond, but the tree we call the Indian almond is a pretender. It is a *jungli* badam, not the real thing. Nevertheless, there are many beautiful and useful things about it, so we love it anyway. Scholarly articles say that this badam has become one of the most common trees in tropical 'littoral habitats' (littoral is a fabulous word for any region that lies along the shore of a sea or a lake), including the Indian coast.

Why is there so much badam along tropical coasts? People plant it there, for one thing, because it is one of the few ornamental trees that can flourish in sandy soil where it is sprayed by salt water and buffeted by strong winds. Secondly, its seed, like the coconut's, is surrounded by a fibrous fruit that can float on water to other coasts, where it takes root.

Cool facts

🍃 The badam tree has a huge wingspan. Once the trunk reaches a particular height, the tree starts putting out branches horizontally. When things are good, these branches can get to be really long! Each of these l-o-n-g branches carries a number of l-a-r-g-e leaves, which makes the badam a lovely tree to shelter under when the sun is beating down.

🍃 Silkworms that produce the silk thread that is woven to make tussar silk love feasting on badam leaves. (Does anyone in your family own a tussar silk saree? Find out!)

🍃 The Indian badam is one of the few tropical trees that is deciduous (leaf-shedding). Just before the leaves drop off, they turn bright red. Until about sixty years ago, Brazil had a lot of Indian badam trees planted along the avenues of its big cities—the government thought the 'fall colours' of the badam's leaves gave their cities a decidedly European flair!

How to recognize a jungli badam

Look for leaves that are large and 'ovoid' or egg-shaped, and branches that start a long way up the trunk and grow outwards, parallel to the ground. When it is leaf-fall season, you can spot the badam a mile away, from the flaming colours of its leaves.

Where you can spot them

In littoral regions, of course, and on streets and in parks everywhere, especially in Maharashtra, West Bengal, and the five south Indian states.

AMALTAS

Summer's Golden Shower

In late April, just as the searing Indian summer explodes over north India, the streets, parks, and college campuses of our capital city of New Delhi turn into gold as the amaltas, or Indian laburnum, bursts into bloom. Hanging upside down like beautiful floral chandeliers, the clusters of fragrant yellow flowers make a heart-lifting sight.

Because the amaltas is one of the world's loveliest flowering trees, its origins are hotly debated, with everyone, including the Greeks and Egyptians, claiming it as their own. However, it has now been more or less firmly established that the amaltas is Indian—hooray!

Cool facts

🍃 The amaltas' cylindrical seed pod can grow as long as 2 ft! Inside is a sweetish, pulpy substance that is used as a safe and effective laxative for humans.

🍃 By the time the seed pod falls off the tree, still tightly closed, its shell has turned very hard. How do the amaltas seeds get out of that seed pod, then? It was British forestry expert Robert Scott Troup who performed a famous experiment around 1905 in Dehra Dun and discovered the answer—jackals! Yes, it was jackals—as well as bears, boars and monkeys—who cracked open the hard shell to get at the pulp, swallowed the seeds along with it, and then passed them out of their digestive systems somewhere else in the forest, where the seeds took root and grew.

How to recognize an amaltas

By its long, cylindrical seed pods, which hang off the tree in dozens, and are easily spotted because they appear when the tree has shed its leaves. By its young leaves, which start off coppery brown and droopy, before they turn green and strong. And, in the season, by its golden flower showers, of course!

Where you can spot them

All over India, growing in the wild and planted in cities, especially in the capital city. When Kerala celebrates the harvest festival of Vishu in April, the blooms are not just on trees but also in markets, for the amaltas flower—*kanikonna* in Malayalam—is the official flower of the festival. It is also the state flower of Kerala.

What's in a Name? Plenty!

Here is a list of the twelve Indian trees that make up our **Desi Dozen**. What are these trees called in Hindi? Kannada? Urdu? Gujarati? Bengali? And your mother tongue? Ask family and friends to help you find the names of these trees in at least three Indian languages and fill up the table!

As an additional fun exercise, find out each tree's scientific name, and write those down as well, in a separate table.

TREE	LANGUAGE 1	LANGUAGE 2	LANGUAGE 3	LANGUAGE 4
Banyan				
Peepal				
Tamarind				
Khejdi				
Neem				
Palash				
Deodar				
Kapok				
Teak				
Jack				
Badam				
Amaltas				

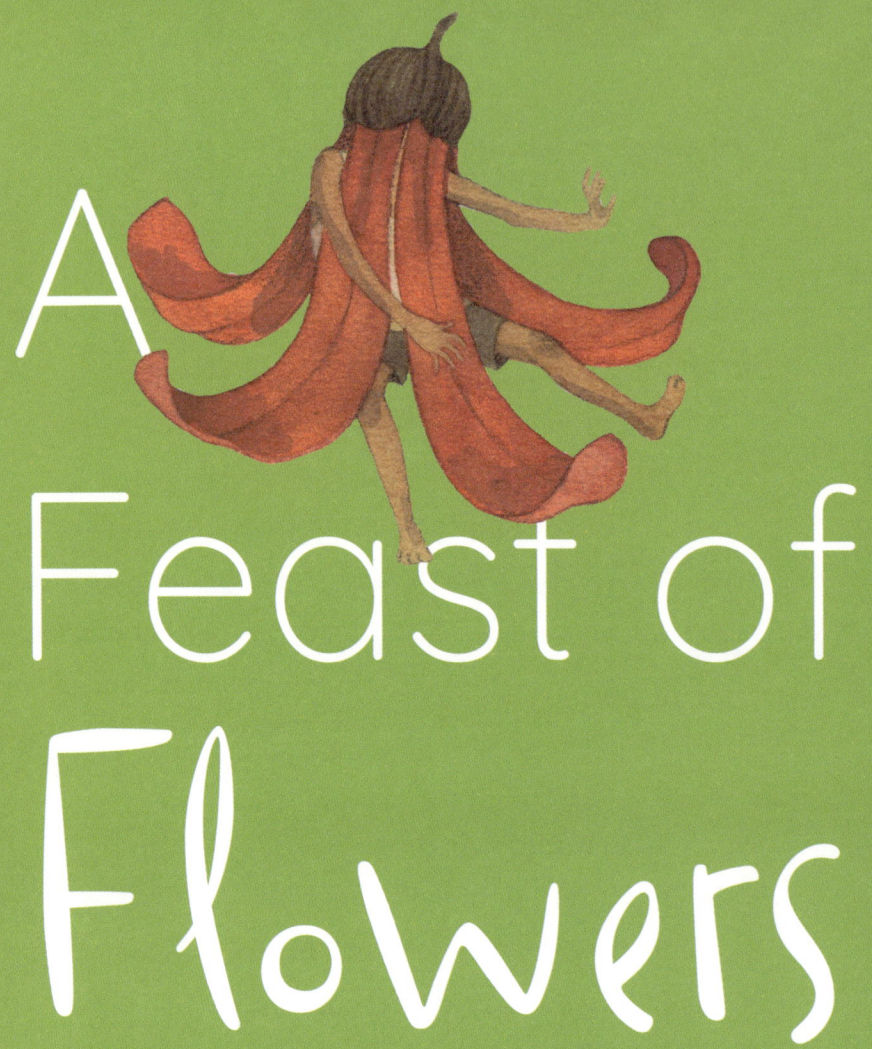

A Feast of Flowers

Through all the noise and pollution of our city streets, if there is one sight that can instantly lift our spirits and make us smile, it is the sight of a tree in flower. Fortunately for us, city planners through the ages have done their best to ensure that flowering trees are planted along large avenues.

Here's a question, though: do trees grow flowers in all those fabulous colours, and scent the air with their delicate, sometimes heady, odours, for *our* benefit? Not at all! Flowers are a tree's 'pollinator magnets', and as we will see on page 123, a tree needs a plethora of insects, birds and other pollinators to help it make seeds, which can then grow into new trees.

Here is a selection of flowers from some of the most common flowering trees found in Indian cities. Some of them, as you may expect, are native to India. But many others have been brought here from very far away because someone fell in love with them and carried them back, to plant here. Now they have become so common that we think of them as Indian trees.

Indian flowering trees

1. *Lagerstroemia speciosa* (Pride of India, Jarul)
2. *Magnolia champaca* (Champak, Sampige)
3. *Bauhinia purpurea* (Camel's foot, Butterfly tree)
4. *Saraca asoca* (Sita Ashok)
5. *Erythrina variegata* (Indian coral tree, Tiger's claw, Mullu murukku)

Foreigners on our streets

1. *Millingtonia hortensis* (Neem chameli): Burma
2. *Tabebuia impetiginosa* (Pink trumpet): Amazon rainforest
3. *Delonix regia* (Gulmohar): Madagascar
4. *Spathodea campanulata* (African tulip): Ghana
5. *Couroupita guianensis* (Cannonball tree): Guyana
6. *Kigelia pinnata* (Sausage tree): Mozambique
7. *Samanea saman* (Rain tree): Peru
8. *Jacaranda mimosifolia* (Jacaranda): The Caribbean

Three 'What, Seriously?!' Facts About Trees

FACT 1
Trees Care for Each Other

Do plants have feelings? Can they feel pleasure and pain? And can they sense another's pain and come together to help them? Yes, yes, and yes!

We have always known that plants respond to stimuli—for instance, a plant can 'feel' sunlight, and will always grow towards it. A touch-me-not plant responds to touch by closing its leaves. The large and beautiful raintree, which lines major avenues in many Indian cities, folds its leaves when it rains, and at night, when it 'sleeps'.

But it was the genius Indian physicist and botanist, Jagadish Chandra Bose, who demonstrated in 1901 that plants can also feel pain. First, he hooked up a plant to a machine he had invented, which could measure the electrical signals the plant was giving out. He then placed the plant's roots in a jar of poisoned water. The scientists who were gathered there watched in horror as the plant's 'pulse' stuttered wildly before it stopped entirely. The plant had clearly suffered before it died! In other experiments, Bose showed that plants grew strong and healthy when they were talked to lovingly (DO try

this at home) and did badly when they were spoken to harshly.

In 1990, a Canadian research student called Suzanne Simard went underground (literally!) and discovered something completely magical—mycorrhizae! Myco-*what*? A close and warm friendship between fungi and tree roots, that's what! Simard found that the roots of forest trees had been entirely taken over by fungi, but the relationship between the two was a very cordial one.

Since fungi do not have chlorophyll and cannot make their own food, the tree's roots brought them sugars to feast on. In return, the fungi, using their thin, long tubes called hyphae (say *high-fay*), went far and wide in the soil to find nutrients that the tree's roots could not reach and fed the roots with it. Win-win! The fungi also stored extra sugars and nutrients to help trees and saplings around them stay alive in times of trouble, like during a drought or a long frost.

There's more. The fungi and their hyphae, Simard found, formed the underground communication system of the forest! When a predator—a gaur or a chital or a caterpillar—nibbles at a leaf, the leaf sends out electrical signals that tells the rest of the tree's leaves to start putting out nasty-tasting chemicals so that the predator does not linger too long. Under the earth, urged by the tree, the fungi pick up these signals and pass them along their hyphae to other tree roots, warning *those* trees to protect themselves. Wow. We think trees cannot 'speak' because we cannot hear them, but they chatter constantly on their mycorrhizal hotlines to take care of each other!

Oh, one last thing. Someone in the renowned science journal, *Nature*, came up with a very clever name for the underground mycorrhizal system. They called it the... Wood Wide Web! Needless to say, the name has stuck.

FACT 2
Trees Control the Climate

Do forests grow in places that receive a lot of rain, or does rain fall plentifully where there are forests? Even though people have always believed that the latter is true, scientists scoffed at that view. They said rain came from the ocean. As water evaporated from the ocean, the water vapour gathered into clouds. The wind blew these clouds towards land, bringing us rain. This is true, of course, but is it the ONLY truth? If it were, we should not have forests growing thousands of kilometres away from the ocean, because the ocean clouds would have dropped all their rain before they got there. But there are many forests growing deep inland.

How come?

The answer is a phenomenon called the 'biotic pump'. Sure, there is more water in the ocean than in a forest, but a forest has many, many leaves, and grass, and moist soil, all of which are 'sweating', or giving out water vapour, through the day. This water vapour rises to the cool atmosphere high above the forest, where the vapour turns back into water and forms clouds. To fill the vacuum this creates, the forest sweats some more,

and more clouds are formed. This vertical loop continues until most of the water vapour from the forest is gone.

NOW what does the forest do to fill in the vacuum above it? Easy—it pulls in moisture from its surroundings, i.e., it pulls in air carrying water vapour from the ocean, towards itself! A forest actually 'attracts' rain, and in that way, controls the climate!

Let that sink in for a minute. Now imagine what happens when large swathes of forest are cleared for humans to build on or plant crops. Climate change, what else?

FACT 3
Trees Have Inspired Citizen Movements

9/11. Nine-eleven. When you hear those numbers, said together like that, what does it bring to mind? If you are old enough to remember the horrific event, or have read about it, or have visited the memorial in New York City, you will instantly think of the 2001 terrorist attack on the World Trade Towers, which left at least 5,000 people dead. On the same date, almost 300 years ago, another terrible massacre happened, in a tiny desert village near Jodhpur called Khejarli.

It was 11 September, 1730. In the Bishnoi village of Khejarli, deep inside the hot and arid Thar desert, the men were away in the fields, and the women were busy with household chores. The Bishnois were (and are) followers of a 15th century saint called Guru Jambheshwar, who gave them 29 [*bees* (20) + *noi* (9) = Bishnoi] rules to live by. Eight of those rules were about conserving and protecting the animals and trees that shared the harsh landscape with them. Of the trees in the Thar, the khejdi (see page 68) was the dearest and most sacred to the Bishnois.

That fateful morning, Amrita Devi Bishnoi was cooking lunch for her three daughters when she heard hoofbeats thunder up to her village. She rushed outside, and found herself face to face with the soldiers of Maharaja Abhay Singh of Jodhpur. They were collecting wood from all over the countryside for the building of the Mehrangarh Fort, and they were at Khejarli to chop down all the trees in the khejdi grove.

Amrita Devi's heart sank. She would never, never allow anyone to cut down her beloved khejdis. She pleaded with the soldiers, but they would not listen. Determined not to let the soldiers have their way, she threw her arms around the nearest tree and hugged it tight. Swish! Down came a soldier's axe, separating Amrita Devi's head from her body and cutting through the khejdi in one smooth movement.

All hell broke loose. Amrita Devi's daughters, reeling with shock, nevertheless threw their young arms around three other trees, and were ruthlessly slaughtered for their pains. The news spread like wildfire through the surrounding Bishnoi villages. Bishnois poured out of their villages, prepared to sacrifice one Bishnoi life for every tree if they had to. By the end of the day, no less than 363 trees—and 363 Bishnois—had been massacred.

When the Maharaja heard what had happened, he was overcome by grief and remorse, and filled with admiration for the courageous Bishnois. He immediately issued a decree forbidding the cutting of trees and the hunting of animals around Bishnoi villages. That decree is honoured to this day.

In India today, September 11 is celebrated as National

Forest Martyrs' Day. On this day each year, the Amrita Devi Bishnoi National Award is awarded to a champion of wildlife conservation.

Amrita Devi did not die in vain. Two hundred and sixty-three years later, in 1973, her sacrifice inspired the Chipko Movement, independent India's first and largest forest conservation movement. It was led by feisty women who loved their trees and were aghast at the kind of deforestation that was happening in the Garhwal Himalayas (in today's Uttarakhand).

The flashpoint for the Chipko Movement came at Reni village on 25th March 1974. In an eerie echo of history, the men of the village were away at the time, and it was the women, led by a braveheart called Gaura Devi, who came out to protect the trees from the loggers. Once again, the loggers did not listen to the women's pleas; once again, the women threw their arms around the trees (*chipko* means 'stick' in Hindi—the women stuck themselves to the trees through the night). Fortunately, this time, the loggers did not react like the king's soldiers. They simply left the next morning, frustrated. The women had won!

In 1980, the then Prime Minister, Indira Gandhi, issued a 15-year ban on the felling of trees in the region, until the green cover was restored.

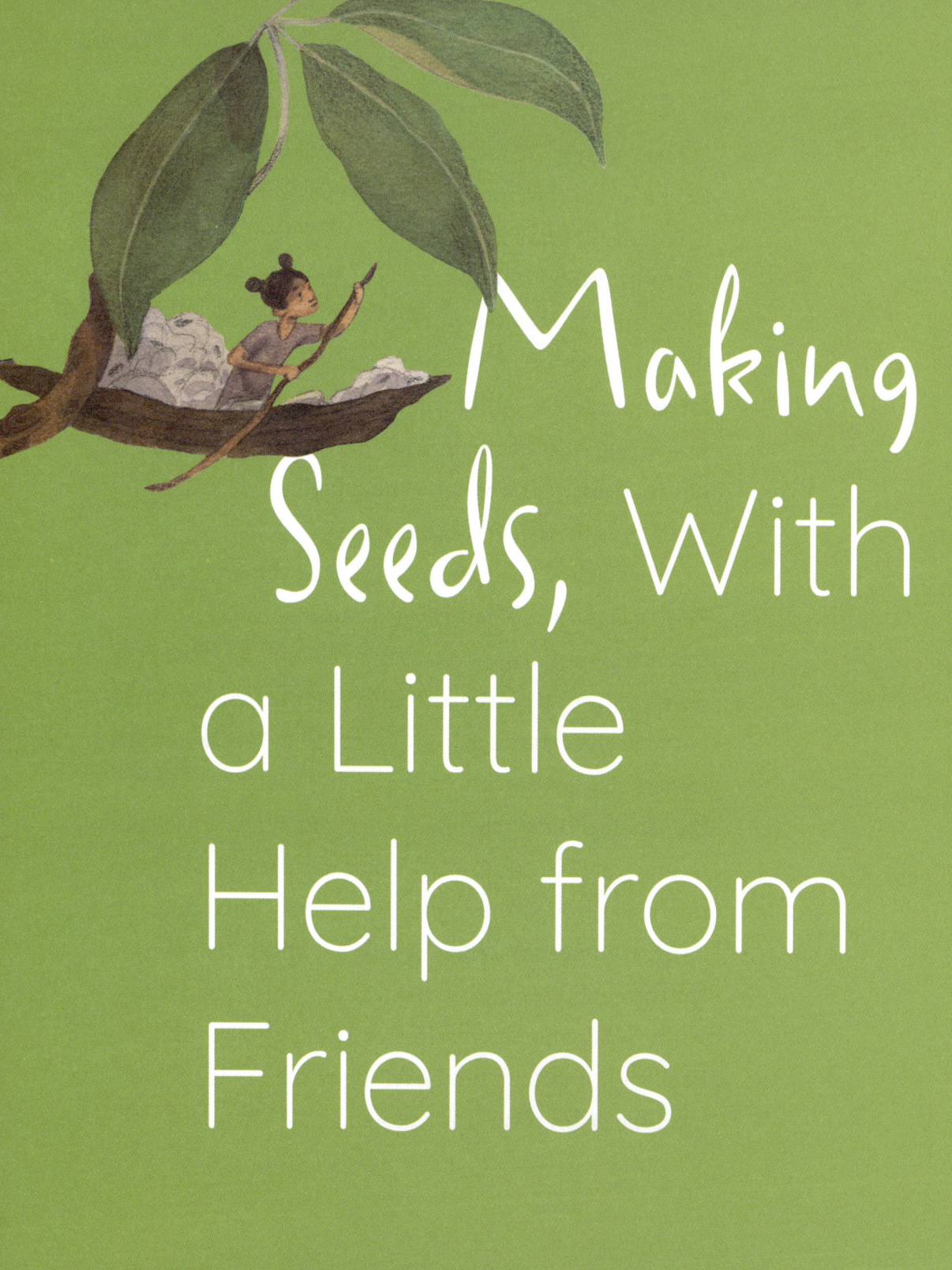

Making Seeds, With a Little Help from Friends

How does a tree make sure that more trees populate the Earth? By making seeds. And how exactly are seeds made? When pollen, the powdery yellow substance produced by a male flower, fuses with the ovules (you can think of them as tiny eggs) waiting inside a female flower, a seed is born. Now, considering that neither trees nor flowers can move, how does the pollen travel from the male flower to the female*? A-ha! *That's* where the pollinators or 'pollen couriers', come in!

Insects like bees, flies, wasps, and butterflies, some birds, and even a few species of bats, attracted by the odour (or colour, or both) of a particular flower, fly into the flower to sip its sweet nectar and feast on its pollen. In the process, their feet and bodies get covered with the yellow pollen dust. When the same insect or bird travels to another flower, some of the pollen drops off and finds its way to the ovules in the female flower. Each time an ovule gets 'fertilized', i.e., fuses with pollen—*ta-daa!*—a seed begins to form!

Around 80% of the world's flowering plants depend on animals for pollination. Most of the others are wind-pollinated, i.e., the wind carries the pollen from one flower to another. For some plants, water is the courier! (Do you think wind-pollinated flowers are colourful

---

*Many flowers, including the rose and the hibiscus, contain both male and female parts in themselves!

How many pollinators can you spot in this picture?

There are at least 13, of which 3 are rather large.

But most are tiny, so look carefully!

and/or fragrant? Why or why not? Now think about bat-pollinated flowers. Would they bloom during the day or at night?)

Once a precious seed is made, the tree builds a safe-keeping case for it. In some trees, these safe-keeping cases take the form of seed pods. In others, the safe-keeping cases take a more delicious, nutritious form—fruit! Many, many fruits* and seeds (including cacao beans, from which chocolate is made) that we enjoy eating would not have been produced at all if not for animal pollinators. Shudder!

* Technically, tomatoes, cucumbers, and aubergines are also fruit, because they have seeds. True vegetables—potatoes, carrots, turnips—do not have seeds. Now you know.

Spreading the Forest: Here Come the Dispersers!

We have talked about how trees do the hard, hard work of producing flowers, attracting pollinators, making seeds, and encasing them in safe-keeping cases. What next? Sending their seeds out into the world, of course!

How do trees make sure their seeds travel? Oh, they have their clever, clever ways, and many of them involve cool seed design.

Here are some of the kinds of seeds trees produce.

🌿 Seeds with wings, sent away on the back of a strong wind

🌿 Seeds that float, carried away by rivers or seas

🌿 Seeds with hooks, which happily hitch a ride on any animal, or human, that passes by.

🌿 Seeds that are buried deep inside delicious fruit. Frugivores (fruit-eating creatures) of all kinds—birds,

The coconut seed is surrounded by fibre that helps it float

The winged seeds of the moringa (drumstick) tree

The xanthium's burred seeds hook themselves to fur and clothes

The balsam's seed pods explode to release seeds

bats, monkeys, elephants and more—devour the fruit, pooping the seeds far away from the mother tree. Wherever the seeds drop, new trees grow, spreading the forest.

🌱 Seeds that BURST out of their pods and are carried far away by the force of the explosion.

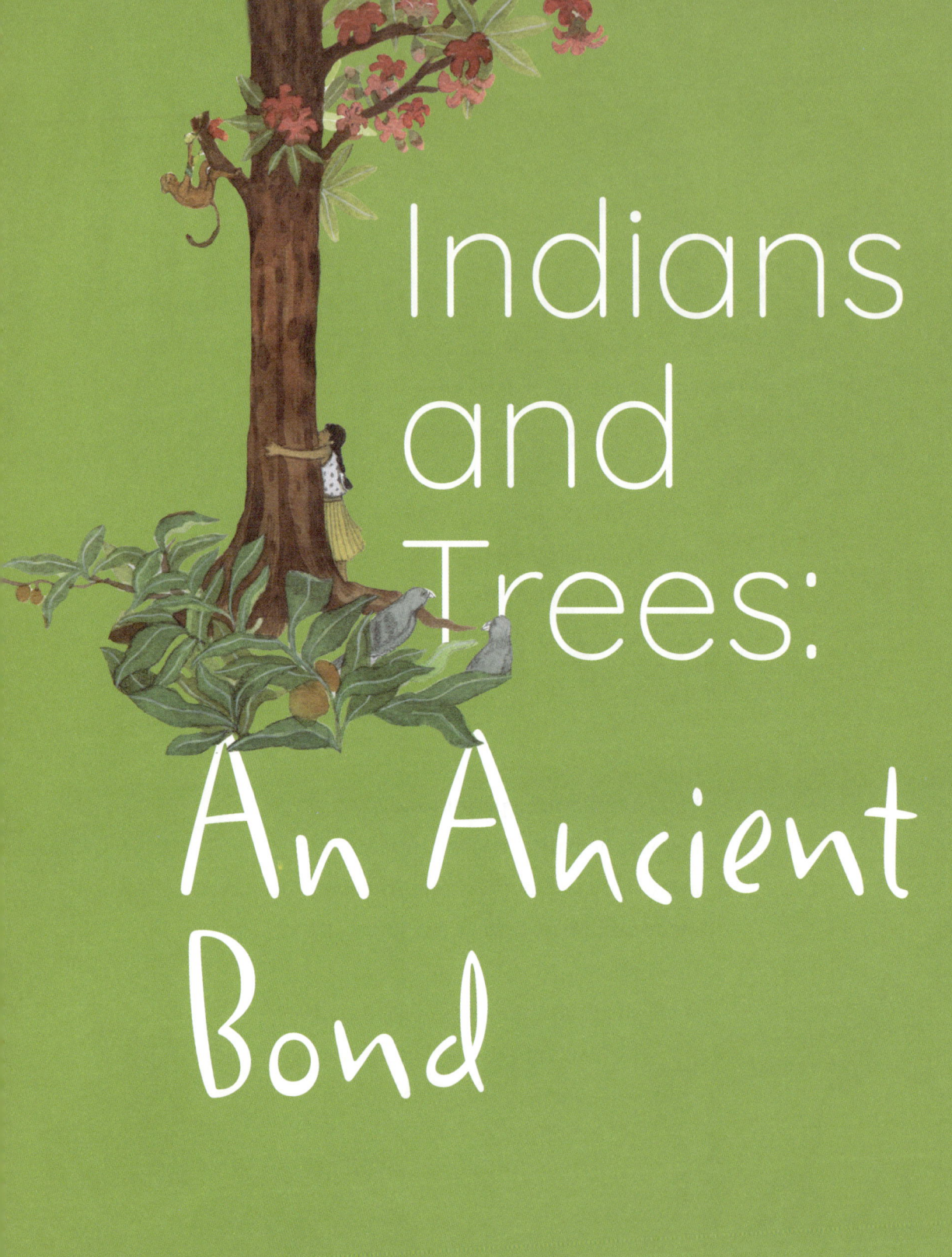

Indians and Trees: An Ancient Bond

Most people acknowledge that trees are wonderful, useful, essential, and soothing to the mind and heart, but India goes one step further. Here, we have always believed that trees—along with animals, birds, insects, wind, water, the earth, the Sun, and everything, living and non-living, that we see around us—are also sacred, the abodes of gods and other divine beings.

This reverence for trees has ensured that our forests remain protected, not only by law but by something far more powerful—the love of common people.* For millennia, traditional communities in India have set aside certain areas of forest as 'sacred groves'. The community protects the grove and does not permit any hunting or logging (cutting down trees for timber) there. Most communities do not even allow people to collect fallen twigs for firewood or wild honey from honeycombs.

How many of these sacred groves do you think there are, all over the country? Over 14,000, and these are only the 'official' ones!

---

*Unfortunately, sacred groves are now under serious threat across India.

Each state and region has a different local name for these groves. In Rajasthan, for example, the Bishnois (see page 118) call theirs *oraans*; in Manipur, they are called *gamkhaps*; in Odisha, *thakurammas*; in Tamil Nadu, *vanakkoil*; in Chhatisgarh, *devgudi*; in Manipur, *ki law lyngdoh*. Kerala has the largest number of sacred groves, or *sarpa kavus*, of any state—no less than 2,000! Maharashtra has about 1,600 *devrais*, and Karnataka 1,464 *devara kadus*. Makes you feel all warm and happy inside, right?

Magical, Mystical, Mag-Ni-Fi-Cent!

Woah! That was quite a journey of discovery through the Treeverse, wouldn't you say? And to think that we have only barely skimmed its surface! No matter—we've made a start, and that's what counts.

What next? Well, getting to know trees even better, that's what! Here are some things that might help.

🍃 Go for a 10-minute 'no-talk quiet walk' in your neighbourhood park at least twice a week, taking long, deep breaths as you stroll along. Don't worry about identifying trees or making notes each time, just enjoy the feeling of being among trees.

🍃 Join organized 'tree walks' in your city whenever you can. Apart from discovering all kinds of cool info about trees, you will also get to spend time with fellow tree lovers on these outings. Always a good thing—you cannot help but become infected by their enthusiasm!

🍃 Buy yourself a good field guide to Indian trees. Sure, there is a lot of great information about trees on the internet, but there is no substitute to having a trusty physical book, written by an expert, by your side. Add a magnifying glass, a (phone) camera, a small knife (to open fallen seed pods or slice through fallen berries and fruit to take a peek inside), your Tree Journal, pencils, crayons (to make bark rubbings), a couple of sample collection bags, and some sanitiser into the mix and you have a Tree Explorer Kit ready! The next time your family is planning a picnic in a public park in your city (if they are not into that kind of thing, nudge them towards it) or a visit to a jungle resort, take the kit along. Your outing just became ten times more exciting!

Whatever you do, stay curious and stay grateful. After all, none of us would be here if not for trees. Let's make sure they know how much we love and appreciate them, with, um, *every breath we take*!

Have fun, young Tree Explorer! The trees are out there, all around you, waiting to love you back!

End Note

'People look at a tree and think it comes out of the ground, that plants grow out of the ground. But if you ask, where does the substance of the tree come from? You find out... that trees come out of the air!'
— Nobel Prize winning American physicist Richard P Feynman

(For Feynman's complete and super fun explanation of how trees come out of the air, scan the QR code above!)

A Note of Gratitude

I never really looked at trees until I was well into my thirties. I could identify the mango leaves that my mum strung across the front doorway at festivals, the banana leaves I ate off at weddings, the curry leaves that went into the tempering of curd rice, and the coconut leaves that my grandmother had the house help strip to their ribs before turning them into sturdy brooms, but little else. I could make diagrams of xylem and phloem for my science teachers, and get full marks on a question about photosynthesis, but point to a tree and ask me to identify it, and I would be entirely clueless.

I didn't even realize what a terrible handicap this was and how much I had been missing until I went on a tree walk with Vijay Thiruvady close to two decades ago. Apart from knowing a LOT about trees, Vijay is also an excellent raconteur who brings together history, mythology, geology, engineering, and a deep love for the Earth and all its creatures, especially trees, into his storytelling. I was mesmerized by the way he talked about trees; by the end of the walk, I was a convert for life. I still know very little about trees, but the spark that Vijay kindled has led me to value trees deeply and look upon them as dear friends.

A couple of years after my life-changing walk, my family and I had the great fortune of going on a nature walk with Karthikeyan Srinivasan, Chief Naturalist, Jungle Lodges and Resorts, on the grounds of the Kabini River Lodge near Mysore. In the span of a couple of hours, Karthik had shown us a teeming universe of tiny creatures that had thus far been entirely invisible to our unobservant eyes—beetles, bugs, insects, spiders, ants... Fascinated, I logged in to his blog, www.wildwanderer.com, and was stunned by the amount of content there, not just about the wee 'uns but also about birds, reptiles, and trees, particularly the flowering trees that make my hometown Bengaluru so beautiful. I have been a fan ever since.

When WWF-India got in touch to ask me if I would like to do a book on trees for children, I jumped at the idea, simply because the opportunity to help children 'see' trees was too valuable to miss. As I mentioned, I am no expert on the subject, but with stalwarts like Vijay and Karthik giving of their time and erudition to review this book, I grew confident to go through with it. For this generosity on their parts, I am immensely grateful.

About Maithili Doshi, the art director on this book, what can I say except what a pleasure it has been to work with someone so experienced but so open to inputs, and so spot on where design is concerned? As for Barkha Lohia, her stunning illustrations are really what make this book the thing of beauty it is; they will go a long way in making children turn their awed gazes treewards.

A big, big thank you to Neha Raghav, Shreya Bhat, and the rest of the team at WWF-India for trusting me with this book, and working so hard to see it through to fruition.

My largest and most unrepayable debt is to the trees themselves, green sentinels who have watched over our Earth almost since its birth, and sustain our breaths—and hearts—in every living moment. Biggggg hugs.

—Roopa Pai

A Note on the Author

Roopa Pai is one of India's best-known writers for children. This computer engineer-turned-author has written over 30 books, ranging from picture books to chapter books and fiction to non-fiction, on themes as varied as sci-fi fantasy, popular science, maths, history, economics, Indian philosophy, life skills, medicine and memoir. Many of her books are bestsellers and are enjoyed as much by adults as by children.

Her best-known books include the eight-part Taranauts, India's first fantasy-adventure series for children in English, *Ready! 99 Must-Have Skills for The World Conquering Teenager (And Almost-Teenager)*, the award-winning national bestseller *The Gita For Children*, listed by Amazon India as one of '100 Indian Books To Read In A Lifetime', and its prequel *The Vedas and Upanishads For Children*. Her most recent book is *The Yoga Sutras for Children*.

Roopa is also a popular speaker—she has spoken at a variety of corporate forums, premier literary events like the Jaipur Literature Festival, international cultural organizations like the Asia Society in New York (at the invitation of the Consul General of India), and international Gita conferences. Her TEDx talk 'Decoding The Gita, India's Book Of Answers'—https://www.youtube.com/watch?v=ckaEwJj2A1U has received over 2 million views to date. She runs short courses online, on the *Gita* and other ancient Indian texts, for children and adults both in India and North America.

Among her books for adults are Indian fitness evangelist and supermodel Milind Soman's award-winning memoir, *Made In India*, and *Cubbon Park: The Green Heart of Bengaluru*, the first-ever history of her city's iconic 152-year-old park. She writes a fortnightly column on Bangalore for the *Hindustan Times*, and has also translated 100 poems of the celebrated Kannada poet, Padma Shri K.S. Nissar Ahmed, into English.

When she is not writing, Roopa leads groups of children and young people on history and heritage walks across her beloved Bangalore and Karnataka, as part of her job as director of a company she co-founded, BangaloreWalks (www.bangalorewalks.com).

About Indian Pitta Kids

Indian Pitta Kids is India's first dedicated children's imprint about nature and wildlife, published in association with WWF-India. Our books will take young readers on exhilarating, informative and funny journeys into the world of the wild.

About Indian Pitta

Indian Pitta Kids is part of the Indian Pitta imprint. Our books about birds and natural history go beyond field/identification guides, to explore the bigger mosaic of habitats, ecosystems and human interactions that touch the lives of birds. Successful conservation programmes, troubling environmental challenges, personal exploration of a landscape, deep dives into the ecology of a species, the quest for a rare species and the sheer joy of birding—these are some of the ideas that you can expect to explore within the pages of our books.

About WWF-India

WWF-India is registered as a Public Charitable Trust. We are an environmental organization with extensive on-ground experience. We combine this knowledge with scientific research and practical insights to create solutions. Our conservation approach is holistic and integrated, connecting wildlife, communities, natural habitats, governments and corporations. This interconnectedness is what makes us unique.